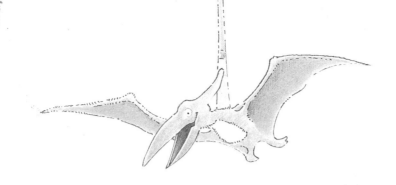

Scholastic Children's Books,
Scholastic Publications Ltd,
7-9 Pratt Street, London NW1 0AE, UK

Scholastic Inc.,
730 Broadway, New York, NY 10003, USA

Scholastic Canada Ltd,
123 Newkirk Road, Richmond Hill,
Ontario, Canada L4C 3G5

Ashton Scholastic Pty Ltd,
P O Box 579, Gosford, New South Wales,
Australia

Ashton Scholastic Ltd,
Private Bag 1, Penrose, Auckland
New Zealand

First published by Ashton Scholastic Ltd, New Zealand, 1990
First published in the UK by Scholastic Publications Ltd, 1991
This edition published, 1992

Text copyright © Mary Carmine
Illustrations copyright © Martin Baynton

ISBN 0 590 55025 X

Printed by Mateu Cromo, Spain

10 9 8 7 6 5 4 3 2 1

DANIEL'S
DINOSAURS

by Mary Carmine

Illustrated by
Martin Baynton

Hippo Books
Scholastic Children's Books
London

Daniel loved dinosaurs.
He loved big dinosaurs
and he loved little dinosaurs.

At the library,
he read books about dinosaurs.
When he drew pictures,
he drew pictures of dinosaurs.

When he wrote stories,
he wrote stories about dinosaurs.

Daniel's dinosaurs were everywhere.
Two Plateosaurs lived next door.

A Segnosaurus sat behind each check-out
at the supermarket.

An Allosaurus directed traffic,
and one unknown variety barked at him
from behind a high fence every morning
as Daniel passed by on his way to school.

Daniel's teacher
was a nice, friendly, plant-eating Diplodocus,
but sometimes . . .

she turned into
a big, fierce Tyrannosaurus!

"I wish you'd think of something else sometimes,"
said Daniel's mother.
"Why don't we go to the city
and visit the Aquarium?"

"That's a good idea," said Daniel.
"I like fish . . .
but not as much as dinosaurs."

It was a long drive to the city.
All the way there,
Daniel drew pictures of dinosaurs.

A smiling Ceratosaurus took their money
at the ticket office.

Daniel and his mother looked at the rock pools,
the sea horses, and the little fish.

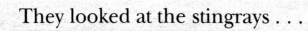
They looked at the stingrays . . .

and stayed for a long time.

They looked at the octopuses . . .

and stayed even longer.

Then they looked at the sharks . . .

and stayed for a very long time indeed.

As they left, Daniel said goodbye
to the smiling, grey nurse shark
in the ticket office . . .

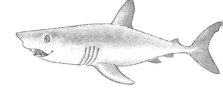

Glossary

Allosaurus (**al**—o—saw—russ)	A meat-eating biped (2-legged), heavily built and slow-moving, up to 12 metres long.
Ceratosaurus (sir—**at**—o—saw—russ)	The only meat-eating biped to have a horn on its nose, the Ceratosaurus was about 6 metres long.
Diplodocus (dip—**lod**—a—kuss)	A plant-eating quadruped (4-legged) and one of the longest known dinosaurs, measuring nearly 28 metres.
Plateosaurus (**plat**—ee—o—saw—russ)	A plant-eating dinosaur, up to 8 metres tall, which walked on either two or four legs.
Segnosaurus (**seg**—no—saw—russ)	A 4-metre long biped with webbed hind toes and a shortish tail, it is thought that the Segnosaurus may have lived by a river and fed on fish.
Tyrannosaurus (tie—**ran**—o—saw—russ)	The 'tyrant lizard', one of the fiercest dinosaurs, the Tyrannosaurus was a meat-eating biped, 14 metres long and 5 metres high, with more than 60 sharp teeth.

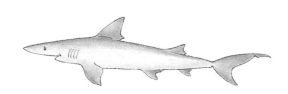

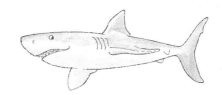